Captain Cayce

By A. Wayne Ross

CreateSpace
7/22/2014

For Cayce

Chapter 1

Gino was more than just a bartender. Gino was Carmine Rizzo's right hand man. He was average in height but broad-chested and with a nose that went every direction but straight owing to his willingness to enforce Carmine's every desire. Gino was not a fighter in the classical sense but he certainly was a brawler. Gino had never backed down from a fight in his life, but had avoided many a fight when the opposition took in his enormous biceps and hands the size of large stones. He normally wore a white shirt with no necktie and traded his black suit coat for a stained white apron when he went behind the bar. This evening Gino has been quite busy making mixed drinks for the diners and cold draft beer for the few people at the bar. The bar was made of fine, highly polished walnut as was the walls of the room. Behind the bar was a huge mirror that allowed Gino to know what was going on even when his back was turned. In fact, Gino and Carmine often secretly gestured to each other through the mirror while Gino had his back to the bar. Subtle little gestures that after years of use meant more than hundreds of words.

This evening Gino gave the mirror an almost imperceptible motion of his head that immediately got Carmine's attention. Carmine glanced in the same direction as the nod, then seeing who Gino was motioning at, he got up from his favorite booth with the red checked tablecloth and meandered over. He pulled his short frame up onto the barstool and reached his beefy hand into the bowl of peanuts setting on the bar. Then Carmine without much effort gave the patron sitting on the next stool a small elbow to the rib cage. The patron slowly turned to face Carmine.

"Carmine, how are you?"

"Probably better than you," Carmine responded, "Is everything okay?"

"Sure."

"And how is your wife?"

"Alright."

"I consider you a friend," Carmine said, "So I'll speak frankly. There is obviously something wrong because it's not like you to sit here and get smashed."

The patron faced Carmine again but said nothing.

"How about I call your wife?"

Again no reply so Carmine made a subtle gesture to Gino who began dialing the phone, then quietly spoke into it. Carmine got up from the barstool and met Gino at the far end of the bar.

Gino whispered in Carmine's ear, "What if he gets unruly?"

"You'll have to do what you always do."

"But, boss, he's a friend."

"Yeah, but you have a job to do."

"The other thing, boss," Gino quietly replied. "They say he can kill a man with just two fingers."

"You're not afraid of him are you?" Carmine asked.

"I'm not afraid of anybody boss. But I'm not anxious to find out if he really can kill someone with two fingers."

Carmine stared at Gino for a minute before saying, "Just keep him happy until his wife gets here. And start watering down his drinks. In fact set a cup of coffee in front of him, maybe he'll drink it."

"Okay boss."

After a few minutes the door to the bar opened, which is separate from the restaurant door even though the two were connected, and the mature but still very pretty woman with the short dark hair entered and strode directly up to the back of the patron still sitting at the bar who was now drinking a cup of steaming hot coffee.

"What are you doing?" she asked.

Without turning to see who was speaking the man said, "Good evening dear. I suppose Carmine called you?"

"No, Gino did."

"Want a drink?"

"No, and neither do you. Get your ass off that barstool and into the car."

"Yes dear," Bobby said as he set the coffee cup down and did as he was told.

A small sigh of relief escaped from Gino as Bobby Morrow wobbled his way out the door leaning heavily on his wife. Carmine approached Gino and asked him, "Any idea what's going on?"

"No boss. I ain't never seen Bobby Morrow get drunk before."

"If he comes back, you better shut him off before someone gets hurt."

Chapter 2

Senator Leonard Snead sat on his butter soft dark brown leather sofa in his richly appointed den staring off into space. The walls in the room were filled with books and photos primarily of the senator shaking hands with famous people or athletes. One photo showed Senator Snead shaking hands with then President Ronald Reagan next to a picture of him standing on the green with Tiger Woods. Row after row of photos, but the senator was just staring out into space, his mind heavy with thoughts of his recently deceased best friend Senator Richard St.Clair of Pennsylvania, and how it could have been him now six feet underground instead of Richard. Both Senator Snead and Senator St.Clair were at a meeting with President Obannon at Camp David when Senator St.Clair was killed by a Secret Service agent who was aiming to kill Bobby Morrow, the former federal undercover agent, when Senator St.Clair jumped in front of Bobby to take the bullet for him. Repayment of a debt carried forward from when Bobby and Richard St.Clair were in the jungles of

Vietnam and Bobby saved his life not once but on several occasions. A debt that Richard St.Clair felt compelled to pay. And he did, with his life. The same life that Bobby saved Richard gave up to repay the debt that Bobby did not even consider a debt. To Bobby it had been an honor to do his duty to such a high standard. Competing with those thoughts were questions surrounding Senator Snead's recent meeting with the committee that he chaired, the prestigious Armed Services Committee and the disturbing news he had just received that Iran had indeed acquired not only the ability to make a nuclear bomb but also the materials required. Since Russia had been dismantling their arsenal of weapons per the new treaty with the United States, some radioactive materials have not been accounted for. It was now common knowledge that some unsavory characters in Russia had managed to get their hands on it and it was going to the highest bidder. Such was the new capitalism in Russia. Anything could be had for the right price. The only obstacle that Iran now faced was former President Reagan's "star wars" defense system. The satellites circling the globe that would stop a ground fired missile with a missile of its own to destroy it before it could reach the United States. That still was not much comfort to the Senator as that system had never been tested. What if it didn't operate as it should? What if it was a useless piece of metal circling the globe?

Bobby Morrow had spent the day in the woods hunting. Dressed in his bright orange hunting coat while he took his gun for a walk as his mind wasn't really on the job at hand. Bobby was depressed. His best friend Richard St.Clair was dead. His federal undercover job was gone. Life looked rather bleak for Bobby. He was stumbling through the woods fooling himself into thinking he was hunting when in actuality he was scaring every animal within three hundred feet of where he was.

Bobby was an excellent hunter and normally could make his way through the woods without making a sound. Without so much as stepping on a small twig to have it snap under the weight and spook the forest critters. Silent as an Indian, normally. But not this day. After a while he got bored and stuck his rifle in his old beat up red pickup truck and headed up the mountain to Rizzo's bar and restaurant. He wasn't interested in eating so he went in the door that took him directly into the bar.

When Bobby entered the establishment, Gino was at his usual place behind the bar and looked up as soon as Bobby entered. He immediately shot a glance over to Carmine who was sitting in his normal booth with the newspaper spread out in front of himself. Carmine saw Bobby come in also and when Gino glanced in his direction, Carmine gave him the signal that Gino was not to serve him any alcohol.

"Gino," Bobby said as he pulled himself onto the red leather covered barstool, "Whiskey, please."

Gino said nothing but went and got Bobby a drink which he sat down in front of him.

"This is coffee, Gino."

"Yeah."

Bobby turned to look at Carmine. Carmine met his gaze and was ready to reply.

The door to the bar flung open quickly slamming into the wall. Everyone looked to see what the commotion was. Two men in stocking masks holding pistols in front of themselves stormed into the bar. The first man immediately smashed Bobby in the side of the head and he tumbled off the barstool and lay motionless on the floor. The man then pointed the pistol at Gino who was moving to reach the gun hidden under the bar. Gino was just pulling the sawed off shot gun out from under the bar when the pistol in the man's hand barked and red quickly spread over the front of Gino's shirt. The second man passed the first man and as Carmine was attempting to get his bulky body out of the booth, the second man shot him. Carmine fell back into the booth. The first man ran behind the bar and rang the cash register. He was stuffing all the money into his pockets. The second man stood guard, watching, scanning back and forth looking for any movement, but the others in the bar were frozen in fear. Never had anyone before dared to rob Carmine. Did these half-wits not know who Carmine was? Carmine's other men, hearing the guns go off, ran from the kitchen with their weapons ready. Spying the man at the register Carmine's man shot him. Not once. Not twice. But numerous times because nobody came into Carmine's place causing trouble and left any other way than in a body bag accompanied by the coroner. The second man didn't wait around for his friend when the recruits poured out of the kitchen. He beat feet for the door staying crouched over to be a much smaller target as he now feared for his life. He instantly went from being the hunter to being the hunted. One of Carmine's men stopped beside Carmine to check on him. He was still breathing. The man pulled out his cell phone and called 911. The second of Carmine's men from the kitchen ran out the door and got a couple shots off at the vehicle that was speeding out of the parking lot spraying gravel as it spun from side to side. Glass shattering as some of the bullets reached their destination but the vehicle kept going and Carmine's man went back into the bar to check on Gino. Bobby was just gaining consciousness on the floor of the bar when the sirens screamed outside and police and ambulance arrived.

Chapter 3

"I want to make sure I have this correct in my report," Chief Galen Farr said to Bobby, "A masked bandit came into Carmine's bar and knocked out the former federal undercover agent, and if the truth be known, probably a government paid assassin, and for sure a hunter of enemies of our government? How does that happen to someone in your position? I'm told you are the best. I've even heard rumors that you have the ability to kill a man with just two fingers."

Bobby sat staring straight ahead, sipping his coffee.

"Come on Bobby," the Chief said, "How does someone get the drop on you?"

Bobby slowly turned to face Galen, "Guess you slow down a little in retirement."

"Guess you do. So I assume you can't provide me with any description of the one that got away?"

Bobby started to rise from the barstool, reached into his pocket, pulled out several dollar bills and tossed them on the counter, then looked directly at Chief Galen Farr and said,

"Galen, I'm sure once you pull the mask off the guy bleeding all over Carmine's floor, that you'll be able to quickly find out who he is and then find out who he runs with. The problem you have Galen, is getting to the other guy before Carmine's guys do. I seriously doubt that Carmine and his guys are going to let this go unpunished. So instead of throwing barbs at me you might want to get your act together and do your job."

Bobby walked towards the door.

"Who said you could leave?" Galen spat at Bobby's back.

Bobby stopped, turned to look at Galen, smiled and continued on his way.

"Get the mask off that idiot on the floor," Galen yelled at his officers.

"The paramedics aren't done with him yet, Chief."

"He's dead. There isn't anything they are going to do for him. Now who the hell is he?"

One of the officers knelt down next to the body and pulled the mask off his face. The officer gasped and looked at the other officer standing and watching. They both looked to the Chief.

"Well? Do you know him?"

The officers looked at each other and in unison said, "Yeah, we know him."

"Well who the hell is it?"

Bobby turned onto his gravel driveway leading up to the large log house which was majestically perched on the crown in the field surrounded by the lush green grass and bordered by trees on three sides. As Bobby made his way up the driveway he could see Sarge's shiny new pickup parked near the house. Then he noticed Sarge and Claire sitting together on the swing talking and laughing.

Bobby got out of his old red beat up pickup truck and sauntered over to the couple on the swing. He sat on the porch rail.

"What did I miss?" Bobby asked.

"You tell him Sarge," Bobby's wife, Claire said, "It's your news."

Bobby looked at Sarge.

"I'm getting married," Sarge burst out with a huge smile on his face.

"You're what?" Bobby exclaimed.

"You heard me, I'm getting married."

"I didn't even know you were dating," Bobby said.

"For a little while now, but we both decided there was no reason to wait."

"So who is it? Anyone I know?" Bobby asked.

"You know her," Sarge said smiling, "Senator Snead's daughter."

"You two couldn't have been dating very long!"

"Don't start acting like my mother," Sarge said, "we might not have been dating very long, but we've dated long enough to know that we love each other."

"So when is the big day?"

"Actually we are eloping. In two days."

"Eloping? Does the Senator know?"

Sarge looked at his watch and replied, "He probably does by now."

"Where are you running off to?" Bobby asked.

"Going to Aruba."

"That sounds really romantic," Claire said.

"That was her idea. I don't care where we go."

"I know I'm not your father, Sarge, but I have to ask," Bobby said, "You and I just lost our jobs. How are you going to support her."

"I landed a great private security position last week. That was one reason why we decided to go ahead and get married. I'll be making really good money and we are going to move to the D.C. area."

"Wow, you're overloading me with news," Bobby replied.

"So where have you been?" Sarge asked Bobby.

"I was up at Carmine's."

With that Claire got up from the swing and went into the house letting the screen door slam shut behind her.

Sarge glared at Bobby, "Whoa man! You are in some deep shit!"

"Yeah just a little."

"What happened to your head. It looks like it's bruised."

"It should be. It hurts like hell."

"What happened?"

I was sitting at Carmine's, minding my own business, having a cup of coffee." The last part he said loudly so his wife would hear him."Anyway, I'm sitting there drinking coffee. Someone bursts through the door and whacks me in the head knocking me out for a minute and completely off the barstool."

"You mean this just happened?"

"Yeah, Chief Farr just let me go a minute ago."

"What else happened?"

"Apparently two idiots tried to rob Carmine. They shot Carmine and Gino."

"Are they okay?"

"They are going to live. You know those two. They're too stubborn to die."

"And I missed all the excitement. Do they know who it was?"

"Probably by now, but I didn't stick around to find out."

"Carmine will be pissed."

"One of them is dead. Carmine's guys shot one of them. The other one got away."

"He better hope he can run long and hard. Carmine is not going to let this go," Sarge said.

"Yeah, old Carmine is like a junk yard dog when you cross him."

"A junk yard dog with rabies!"

Carmine woke up in the hospital connected to beeping monitors by wires and tubes, and surrounded by doctors, nurses, police, and several of his bodyguards.

"What the hell is going on?" Carmine asked gruffly.

"You've been shot," A doctor said.

"I know that! Don't you think I can feel it. Where's Gino? How is he? Is he alright?"

"For right now Mr. Rizzo, I need you to be calm and get some rest," The Doctor said.

"Doc, shut up. You," Carmine said as he pointed to one of his bodyguards, "Where's Gino?"

"Down the hall, Boss. He's okay. Took a bullet in the shoulder."

"Doc, whoever is in the next bed here, you get them the hell out of here and you get Gino moved into this room."

"I can't..."

"Do it Doc, or else."

"Look Mr. Rizzo. I don't take orders from you."

"Guido, find us an ambulance. Me and Gino are getting the hell out of here."

"But Mr. Rizzo," the doctor pleaded.

"Get Gino in this room or we take an ambulance ride. That's not open to discussion Doc." Carmine looked around the room, "And the rest of you people get the hell out of here. My guys and I need to talk."

"But,..."

"Doc, if I have to tell you one more time, I'm going to have Guido there beat it into your head. Scram!"

The room cleared out including the police officers that apparently figured now was not a good time to question Carmine. Two nurses began unhooking the wires and bags from Carmine's neighbor and pushed his bed out into the hall. In just a few minutes another bed with the big beefy body of Gino was wheeled in next to Carmine.

"Gino," Carmine asked, "How you feeling?"

"I'm okay, how about you, boss?"

"I'm gonna' live, which is too bad for somebody."

"Guido, who were those two jokers?"

"The one full of lead and bleedin' all over your floor was that Stallone kid from Ganister."

"A local kid was dumb enough to try to rob us? What about the other one?" Carmine asked.

"The other one got away in Stallone's truck. I've already put out the word, we'll have him soon."

"Good," Carmine said, "I want everyone to know you don't live long robbing my place, but at the same time, be sure the cops can't trace it back to us. You understand?"

"I got it boss. Don't worry, I'll handle it."

"You're a good man Guido."

"Gino, how's come you was so slow with the shotgun? You gettin' old?"

"I guess so Boss."

"Yeah, we both are getting' old. This is a young man's game. Maybe we should retire?"

"Whatever you say Boss."

"I'm just messin' with ya'. What the hell else would we do?"

"We could retire to Florida, Boss."

Carmine looked over at Gino, "I don't even want the thought in my head of you walkin' the beach in Florida wearing a Speedo. Damn, now I probably won't be able to eat dinner. Guido, when's dinner?"

"I don't know what time they come around Boss."

"I ain't eatin' this hospital crap. You have the boys make us some good pasta and bring it in here. Don't forget a nice bottle of wine."

"You got it Boss."

Chief of Police Galen Farr left the crime scene in a hurry. The red and blue lights on the roof of his patrol car were flashing as he fishtailed his way out on to the highway with the tires squealing as they fought the losing battle to grip the asphalt. Farr drove back into Ganister and went through every stop sign on the way to his home where he quickly stopped the car without worrying whether it was off the street so other vehicles could get by. He rushed into his home and on the way into the kitchen was yelling for his wife.

She stood from placing a baking sheet in the hot oven and dusted the flour off her hands onto her apron. Her face was white as she feared the worst from having her normally quiet husband yelling as he crashed through the door.

"Galen," she asked in a panic, "What's wrong?"

"Where's Troy?"

Troy was Galen's son. Recently graduated from high school and supposedly looking for that first job while he contemplated if college was the path he should follow.

"He's out with his friends, I assume."

"Is he with that Stallone kid?"

"Well Mick came by here earlier and they left together , why?"

"How many times have I told you to not let him run around with that punk?"

"He seems like a nice boy, Galen."

"Well, then, he *was* a nice boy."

"Galen, what do you mean?"

"I mean he's laying dead in a pool of blood at Rizzo's restaurant."

Galen's wife pulled out a kitchen chair and plopped down on it. Her hand involuntarily covered her mouth as she gasped and asked Galen, "Oh no Galen, what happened?"

"Seems the Stallone kid and someone else tried to rob Rizzo's Restaurant."

"Are you sure?" Galen's wife asked.

"Yes, I'm sure. I saw the body."

"And he's dead?" she asked her breathing becoming labored.
"Dead as a doornail. Lying there in a pool of his own blood."
"How did that happen?"
"You just don't waltz into Carmine's place and expect to rob
him without consequences. Everyone around here knows he
has mafia connections. What kind of idiot would do that?"
"Galen, where is Troy?"
"That's what I'm asking you?"
"You don't think he had anything to do with a robbery do
you?"
"I'm a cop. I suspect everybody. And they were friends, you
said yourself they left here together."
"Oh no...." Galen's wife said as she broke down crying. Huge
warm tears flowing from between her fingers and dropping
onto the freshly mopped kitchen floor.
"I have to go," Galen said as he turned away from his wife, "If
Troy comes in you call me immediately."
Galen's wife was still crying.
"Do you hear me?" he asked her again.
She nodded her head without looking up. The dreaded
possibility of one of a parent's worst fears working its way
into her mind. The tears flowing even harder now.

Chapter 4

Senator Snead was spending the day working from home. Reports from every branch of the military and the alphabet agencies like the FBI, NSA, HSA, and many more scattered across his desk as he attempted to assimilate all the data into precise thoughts and insights necessary for him to do his job and keep the country safe from foreign countries, druglords, crackpots, and terrorists. As the chairman of the Armed Services Committee he had a tremendous need to know about any and all incidents that may be brewing. And when the President asked a question, it would not look good if he were not aware of an incident no matter how large or small. Most recently there was the kidnapping of the freighter captain by pirates off the coast of Somalia. Senator Snead had no sooner read the report when the President had called and asked him for more information even though the President then stalled and did not want to pursue the military approach to capturing the pirates and getting the captain back, that was outlined by Senator Snead and his top military brass. As the Senator studied all the reports the news channel was blaring in the background, and even though the Senator didn't appear to be listening, whenever any comment came up that was useful to the Senator he would stop reading and face the television. Leonard was swearing at the television when the door opened and his daughter, Sadie strolled in. Not checking on whether her father was busy or not, she immediately spoke to the Senator.

"Dad," she said, "We need to talk."

"We'll talk later, honey," the Senator replied without looking up from his work, "I have a lot of work to do first."

"But, Dad," she pleaded with the corners of her mouth turned down, "This is important." Her voice getting higher and higher. Lenny fearing what would come next if he didn't let her have her say forced his to look up from his papers, stared her in the eye, and ask, "Tell me what's wrong, Sadie."

"There's nothing wrong, Dad," she said, "I just need your undivided attention so I can tell you something."

"Sadie, can't you see that I am busy?"

"Too busy for your daughter?"

That line never failed to get immediate results. Guilt was the cattle prod of the younger generation.

Leonard sighed, clasped his hands together and laid them down on top of the many papers he had been studying and looked to his daughter.

Sadie smiled. The Senator's heart melted. And the concerns for the country went to the back burner.

"What can I do for you Sadie?"

"Promise me you'll stay calm when I tell you this."

"Tell me what?"

"First you promise to be calm."

"Calm? How can I be calm when you start a sentence like that?"

"Dad," the pouty face came back. "Dad, you promised to listen."

"I'm listening. I'm listening," he said.

Barely unable to control herself, she blurted it out, "I'm getting married."

The Senator tried to gather his thoughts for a minute then asked, "You're what?"

"I'm getting married."

"To who," he asked with a quizzical look on his face, "You're not even dating anybody."

"Sure, I am."

"Who?"

"I've been dating Sarge for several months now."

"Sarge?" Leonard asked, "You mean the big bodyguard that worked here a short while back?"

"Yes, dad. Sarge."

"How the…, Where's your mother? Have you talked with your mother about this?"

"Of course, dad."

"Well what did your mother say?"

"Pretty much what you just said."

"Sadie, don't you think you're rushing into something?"

"No, dad, I don't. And I'm getting married with or without your blessing. I would just rather have your blessing."

"Go find your mother. Get her in here," the Senator said in a low voice as thoughts of surrender started to fill his head.

Sadie left for the briefest of moments and came back with her mother in tow.

Leonard looked at his wife Karen as she slowly meandered into the room being dragged by the arm by her daughter.

"What is going on here?" Leonard asked his wife.

"You know as much as I do," Karen said.

"Shouldn't you be talking her out of this?"

"I'm tired of beating my head against the wall," Karen said sharply, "You talk her out of it."

"I'm old enough to make my own decisions," Sadie snapped.

"I'm not questioning your age," the Senator said, "I'm questioning your judgment."

"This is not open to debate," a defiant Sadie said as she thrust her hands onto her hips, "The only question is if you want to come to the wedding service or not."

"And I suppose you expect me to pay for some over-the-top wedding?"

"As a matter of fact, I, I mean we, don't."

The Senator's mouth dropped open and Sadie continued.

"We are having a small service with just a couple people then we are leaving for Aruba for our honeymoon."

"Aruba?"

"Yes. Aruba."

"Well, I guess you have everything planned," Leonard said, "So what do you need me for?"

"Because I want you and mom to be at the wedding service."

"Whatever your mother decides," the Senator said, admitting defeat and carrying his suddenly weakened body back to his desk chair where he crashed into the seat.

The Senator had no sooner sat down and his phone rang. He picked up the phone.

"Senator Snead?"

"Yes," a dejected Senator replied, "Who's this?"

"Please hold for the Attorney General."

Bobby always enjoyed the early morning hours at his log home, times just like this when he knew Claire was sleeping deeply as he sat on the swing hung at the corner of the huge porch that went around two sides of his magnificent home. The sun had just come up and Bobby was swinging, drinking his extra large mug of coffee, and watching Mother Nature at work. The bumblebees were trying to bore holes into sturdy wood logs that made up the walls of his home, birds flew past with amazing speed and agility heading to the trees at the edge of his property. The one thing missing was his faithful dog. The big black Rottweiler that had provided him so much companionship. The one those assholes killed when they came to kill Bobby. Bobby mentally tried to change channels. To think of something other than that day. Instead his mind went to Sarge. He was just a big muscular grunt when Bobby took him under his wing. Since then he had grown into an intelligent, sensible man. Or so it seemed until he dropped this recent bombshell about eloping with Senator Snead's daughter. But then, Bobby thought, maybe that was an intelligent move for Sarge also. After all, Bobby himself was a much better man for having Claire beside him all these years. And when they met it was "love at first sight", so maybe it would all work out for Sarge. Bobby hoped so. Bobby raised his mug in the air and did a silent toast to Sarge and Sadie. Bobby's thoughts were interrupted by the ringing of his cell phone. Begrudgingly he answered it.

"What's up," was all that Bobby said when he saw the recognizable phone number.

"Bobby," a desperate female voice said, "It's Amy." She sniffed away tears before continuing, "It's the Colonel. He passed away last night."

Amy was the Colonel's loyal secretary. She probably held as many secrets in her head as the Colonel did. The Colonel was at one time exactly that, a Colonel in the Army. Bobby had met him during his tour in Vietnam when the Colonel came to pin one of Bobby's many medals on him. Several of those were for saving the now deceased Senator Richard St.Clair's life which was practically a full time job for Bobby back then. Bobby remembered when the Colonel pinned on the medal. Bobby sharply saluted the Colonel then immediately unpinned the medal and put it in his pocket where it remained until he got into his bunk area and tossed into the shoebox with all the others. One day he got tired of looking at the shoebox and mailed it home. Medals were not going to keep him out of a bodybag here in the jungles of Vietnam so

Bobby had no use for them. After the war, the Colonel contacted Bobby and asked to meet with him. Assuming it was just a friendly gesture Bobby readily agreed and travelled to Washington to meet with the Colonel. The Colonel surprised Bobby with a job offer. The Colonel had become the President's personal intelligence supplier and problem solver. While the president had the FBI, CIA and all the other three letter agencies at his command, the President was wary of how far he could trust them and how accurate the information was so he entrusted that job to the Colonel. When the President had a problem that needed to be solved without attention, he called the Colonel. The Colonel in turn called Bobby. On occasion it even meant using Bobby's sniper skills and taking out a foreign enemy while giving the President deniability. Bobby worked for the Colonel for many years, and for several presidents. Then the republican's lost the White House and the Colonel and Bobby lost their jobs.

"Amy, I'm very sorry to hear that," Bobby said, "Is there anything I can do for you or the Colonel's family?"

"The Colonel had all his arrangements made ahead of time and he wanted you to say a few words at the brief ceremony that will be held at Arlington cemetery."

"You know I'll do anything for the Colonel."

"I'll email you the details," Amy said, "I just wanted to call you in person before you read it in the newspapers."

"Thank you, Amy. What was the cause of death? I know he was diagnosed with a melanoma of some kind."

"He died of a bullet," Amy started sobbing again, "A bullet to the head. They are saying it was suicide."

"What?" Bobby exclaimed.

Between tears Amy said, "The police say it was suicide. You know as well as I do that the Colonel would never do that."

"I'll pack my bags and be in Washington before you know it, Amy. You try to stay strong."

"Thank you, Bobby."

Bobby closed his phone, sat down his coffee mug, and reached his hand up and involuntarily rubbed his chin. He had several days growth of beard. He looked down at himself, his clothes were a mess. He had been spending his time lately drinking and feeling sorry for himself because he no longer was living the exciting federal undercover life. The Colonel would not be impressed. In fact the Colonel would be downright ashamed. Bobby jumped up off the swing and strode into the house and directly into the bathroom.

Chapter 5

Chief Galen Farr scoured every street in the small borough of Ganister and asked everyone he thought might know but he couldn't find his son anywhere. In desperation he decided he better extend his search so he headed for the Blue Hole. The Blue Hole is an abandoned limestone quarry. A huge hole in the ground, big enough to sit several football fields inside it, and full of deep blue water that arrived courtesy of an underground stream. A small stream of water that flowed constantly enough to shut down the quarrying operation and turn it into a favorite spot for locals to swim. Galen turned off of Route 866 shortly after leaving town onto the dirt road that would take him to the Blue Hole. As he rounded the final curve when the Blue Hole came into view he parked at the top of the quarry. He got out of his car and strode the couple feet to the edge of the quarry walls. Looking down into the quarry he immediately spotted his son. Sitting on the limestone edge near the water skimming stones across the flat blue water making circles pop up each time the stone struck the water then glancing back into the air before coming back in contact with the water again forming another circle.

"Troy," Galen yelled at his son, "What the hell are you doing?"

Troy turned his head and looked up at his dad, "Nothing."

"Get yourself up here," Galen said, "I want to talk to you."

Troy tossed one more stone out across the water making three rings. Not a big deal. Anyone could make three rings, it was five or six rings that was hard to do. Troy slowly started up the gravel path that led to the top of the quarry where Galen stood waiting.

Before Troy could cross the top edge, Galen was firing questions at him, "Where have you been?"

Troy spread his arms out to illustrate without saying anything that this is where he had been.

"Don't give me any crap, son," Galen demanded, "I want the truth from you. And I want it now."

"Dad, I've been here."

"You left the house with Stallone."

"Yeah, so what?"

"So were you with him at Rizzo's?"

Troy looked away from his father and back towards the calm blue water.

Galen made his living reading people's body language. He rubbed his forehead and said to Troy, "How could you be so stupid?"

Troy didn't answer.

"Don't you know that Carmine is going to find out you were with Stallone, and he's going to come after you."

"Dad, I didn't know what Mick was up to. He told me it would be blast to pretend we were robbing Carmine just to see what he would do."

"What the hell do you think a mafia kingpin would do when someone enters his business pointing a gun at him? You're an intelligent young man but where the hell is your common sense?"

No response from Troy.

"And Stallone wasn't playing games when he bashed Bobby on the head knocking him off his stool then shooting Gino. I can't believe this. You, the son of the Chief of Police involved in the stupidest thing to ever happen in this town."

"I'm sorry Dad," Troy said as tears sprung from his eyes. Galen grabbed Troy and pulled him close hugging him while tears sprung from Galen's eyes.

"I don't know if I can protect you son."

"But dad, I don't want to go to prison."

"Son, prison is the least of your worries. Stallone is dead. Carmine's people saw to that and they are perfectly within their rights to have killed him. And I guarantee you they are already looking for Stallone's accomplice. They have a reputation. They have to save face. They will hunt you down and they will kill you."

"But dad, I can get away from here and hide from him."

Galen shook his head and stood back from his son, "And yet, here you are, hanging out at the Blue Hole. Skimming stones across Carmine Rizzo's water."

"What?"

"This. Right here, this is Carmine's property."

"Dad, I gotta' get out of here!"

"You can't run from Carmine."

Chapter 6

Pastor Tyme stood in front of the large brick fireplace which covered the one end of Senator's Snead's study, dressed in his simple white frock, holding his worn bible in both hands as he studied the two smiling faces in front of him before saying, "I now pronounce you husband and wife. You may kiss the bride."

Sarge enveloped Sadie in his huge arms giving her a bear-hug while leaning down and kissing her full on the lips. The kiss lasted longer than the people watching expected. When they finally stopped the four persons watching approached them. Senator Snead and his wife Karen, and Terry Lee and his wife Mickey all took turns hugging the bride and shaking hands with the beaming groom.

After congratulations all around, Sarge looked at his watch and said, "Sorry folks, but we have a plane to catch," then he grabbed his new bride in his huge arms and off they went.

"What say we go have a nice meal?" Senator Snead asked Terry.

"Why not."

"I know a nice place not far off. We'll all go in my car."

"Sounds good to me," Mickey said.

"Yes," Karen answered, "And they have a great selection of wine. Which I could sure use."

The couples laughed simultaneously.

From Richmond, the USAir plane with Sarge and Sadie on board flew to Charlotte where the couple changed planes without ever once letting go of each other's hand. Their smiles seemed to be permanently glued to their faces. After a mere four hours in the air from Charlotte, most of which they spent kissing, the plane landed in sunny Aruba. The couple went through Customs, and Immigration and grabbed their suitcases. They walked through the door of the airport into the extremely warm sunshine of Aruba and looked about for the taxis. In front of the doors stood numerous people all holding signs with various names on them to give them special transportation to their hotels. One of the men, a friendly round faced man dressed in what appeared to be a white sailor uniform and sporting a baseball cap with the word "Captain" embroidered on the front of it was holding a sign that said "Sarge & Sadie". Sarge spotted the sign then looked at Sadie and asked her, "Do you think that could be us?"

"Surely there is not another Sarge and Sadie on this small island."

Sarge approached the man and asked, "Are you waiting for us?"

"If you are the Sarge and Sadie that just tied the knot in lovely Richmond, Virginia, then I'm waiting for you," the jovial man said.

"But," Sarge stammered, "How did you know?"

"Connections, son, connections," the man said with a smile on his face. "Tempest fugit!"

"What?" Sarge asked as he grabbed the suitcases plus his new bride and followed the spry older man down the sidewalk to a waiting vehicle where the man opened the trunk and the backdoors to his car.

"I said Time Flies," said the Captain. "Let's get you two to your resort."

As Sarge placed the suitcases into the trunk, the Captain said to him, "You're staying at the Aruba Beach Club, right?"

Sarge eyed him cautiously, "That's right. But how do you know this?"

The jovial man pointed to his own forehead and said, "Kidneys, man, kidneys."

Sarge laughed and got in the backseat of the car beside his beaming new wife while the Captain closed the trunk and got in the driver's seat and started the car. He looked back at the couple in the rearview mirror and said, "You two are going to love Aruba."

"We love it already, the sky is so blue and it's so warm," Sadie said.

"Blue. You haven't seen blue yet Sadie. Wait till you get your first look at the Caribbean Sea. Then you see blue. You'll see so many shades of blue between the Sea and the sky that you'll never forget this lovely island. And you're going to get that first peak in just a minute once we get past the airport."

"You sound American," Sarge said.

"I am. In fact I'm originally from Richmond also," the Captain told him.

"So do you know my father?" Sadie asked.

"Of course I know the Senator."

"So my father arranged for you to pick us up?"

"Not really. He just mentioned that you were coming. I took it upon myself to pick you up. It can be a hassle sometimes getting a taxi. And the way some of those taxi drivers drive these days, you are taking your life in your hands. I wanted to be sure you got to your resort safely."

"Well that's awfully kind of you," Sarge said.

"Well I do have ulterior motives, also," the Captain said as he glanced in the rearview mirror.

"Ohh…."

"I'll show you in a minute. For now, look to your left. There it is. The most beautiful blue water you will ever see in your life. Welcome to Aruba."

The couple gasped as they took in their first sight of the shimmering aqua water of the Caribbean Sea.

"Now this is the downtown area," the Captain said. "And here on the left next to the dutch restaurant is my little office."

"So you have a submarine?" Sarge asked when he spied the sign adorning the front of the small office.

"Yes, that's how I make my living here. I take tourists to the bottom of the Caribbean Sea where you can see all the fish, marine life, sponges, turtles, and if you're lucky even squid and octopus."

"Well Captain," Sadie said, "How can we refuse? We will definitely take your submarine tour."

"Well, thank you. Just a mile up the road here and you will be at your resort. You picked a lovely place to stay. The beach is much wider here than at the high-rise area and you have fewer people to share it with. I don't understand why everyone runs up to the high-rise area."

The couple kept their heads turned to the left all the while watching the Caribbean Sea until they pulled into the driveway of the Aruba Beach Club.

"Well, here you are," the Captain said as he pulled to a stop. The Captain helped Sarge get the luggage then closed his trunk. Sarge attempted to give the Captain a tip, "The rides free young man. I'll take your money when you come to the submarine."

"Well at least tell me what your name is," Sarge asked.

"Captain. Captain Cayce if you want to be formal."

"Well it is a pleasure to meet you Captain," the couple said in unison.

"If you need anything, you just call me. The people at the desk know my number." The Captain tipped his baseball cap, and began singing a little diddy on his way to his car, "Doot, da, de, da, dooty-do…".

Chapter 7

Bobby Morrow was a man of few words which made him an odd choice to deliver the eulogy for his recently departed former boss, the Colonel. Following Bobby's short speech the Marine Corps did a 21 gun salute followed by the playing of Taps and the flag ceremony. The rugged Marines in their neatly creased uniforms crisply folded the American flag that had been draped over the coffin, then, in a tear-jerking ceremony presented it to the Colonel's wife. After the ceremony the guests started to drift away from the burial site and back to their autos. The Colonel's personal assistant, Amy was still drying her tears with a bunched up Kleenex when she caught up to Bobby.

"Are you going to catch the Colonel's killer?" she asked.

Bobby stopped and looked Amy in the eyes, "You know that is not anything I can properly do. Why don't you agree with the police investigators?"

"I've worked closely with the Colonel for many years, Bobby," she said between sobs, "And you know as well as I do that the Colonel would be the last man in the world to ever give up on anything. Suicide would be giving up. The Colonel would fight Melanoma or any other health problem to the very end. Kicking and screaming, that's how he would go. Not quietly sitting at his desk and pulling the trigger on his pistol."

"You're right about that Amy," Bobby said, "It's just that there are lots of more qualified people than me to investigate this."

"Maybe so," Amy said, "But who knew the Colonel better than you?"

"Okay, I'll swing by his office in just a few minutes and take a quick look around," Bobby sighed, "But if nothing jumps out at me then you need to hire a private investigator."

"Thank you for at least taking a look."

"Would you like to ride over with me now?" Bobby asked.

"Sure. I rode here with friends, just let me tell them I'm going with you." Amy scurried away but by the time Bobby reached his car she was only a few steps behind him. Bobby opened the door for her and she slid into the passenger's seat. Bobby walked around the car and gazed out over the green evenly cut grass at the thousands of white crosses that marked the graves. A sense of duty came over him as he got in the car, started it, and pulled out. A duty that he felt he owed all of his fallen military brethren that lie quietly around him.

Bobby pulled into a parking spot at the Colonel's office and they went into the Colonel's office. After a few minutes Bobby sat heavily in the leather chair that faced the Colonel's desk. A chair that Bobby had spent many hours occupying while the Colonel laid out the various details and strategies of the many operations that they undertook. Bobby's eyes kept wandering to the dark blood stain that now spoiled the rich dark oak wood top of the desk. After a minute Bobby looked away taking in every little detail of the office. The desk had sat in an area where the windows formed a partial octagon around the desk. The rich gold curtains to the left of the desk were covered with crimson dots of dry blood. The curtains to the right of the desk were not marked at all. As Bobby absorbed each detail Amy approached him and handed him a set of large photos. Crime scene photos.

"I asked the crime tech if he would give me a set," she told Bobby.

Bobby looked at her then at the photos. It was different when the subject was your colleague. Normally Bobby could study the photos and feel nothing. Today the bile worked its way up his throat. He continued to carefully study each photo. Then he looked through them again. And again. And again, until he could memorize each and every detail. In the back of his head a small thought sprouted that he was unable to clearly bring to the surface. He looked through the photos again.

"Amy," Bobby said, "Who's gun is this?"

"Isn't it the Colonel's?"

"Are you sure?"

"Well, no, I just assumed it was."

"We have to get a look at it," Bobby said, "Do you have any connections at the police department?"

"Don't need any. NCIS will have everything and I'm sure they will be glad to let us have a look."

"Good. Get them on the telephone and make an appointment."

A slight smile crossed Amy's lips, "I knew you would find something."

"We didn't find anything yet, Amy, but I do have a couple questions. Something is not right here."

"I tried to tell you that. The Colonel would not commit suicide."

"We need evidence Amy. Speculation won't do us or the Colonel any good."

Chapter 8

Chief Galen Farr had barely put his foot across the threshold of the hospital room when Gino and Carmine instantly opened their eyes and looked his way.

"Sorry, " Galen said, "I didn't mean to wake you."

"What brings you here, Chief?" Carmine asked looking as though he were part of a plate of pasta with all the monitors and IV's attached to himself.

"I wanted to see how you were doing."

"What else?" Carmine inquired.

"Well, I guess to see if you have gotten any leads on the accomplice," the chief said quietly.

"I thought that was your job," Carmine snapped back.

A flustered chief responded, "Oh, yes, yes, we are making progress with the investigation."

"Really, chief?" Carmine asked, "Then who do you have for suspects?"

Galen's face reddened, "No actual suspects yet, but…"

Carmine interrupted, "Let me tell you a little story." Not waiting for a response he continued, "There was this little boy on an airplane reading a magazine. He noticed that the man next to him was the same man that was featured in the magazine article so he asked the man, 'why should people vote for you to be their Senator?'"

The man looked at the small boy and smiled his big toothy grin and replied, "Well son, because I'm the best man for job."

"Really?"

"Well sure son. I take good care of my constituents and have only their best interests at heart."

"So you must be really smart?"

"Well, yes, I guess you could say that," the man said with a smile.

"But to help people you would have to know about lots of different things?"

"Yes, son, you would. And I do. I'm an educated man," he said. Then he asked the boy, "Would you vote for me?"

"Maybe, but first I would have to ask you a question."

"Well, then, by all means, ask me a question."

"How's come cows and rabbits both eat grass, but cows make great big sloppy patties when they go to the bathroom and yet bunnies just make little round balls?"

"Well I don't really know the answer to that son."

The boy then said, "Well then I wouldn't vote for you."

"Why not?"

"Because you don't know shit."

Carmine then said to the chief, "Get my meaning chief?"

"Your meaning is crystal clear Carmine."

"Another thing chief," Carmine said with a smile, "Don't come sniffing around here thinking we are going to do your job for you. Do your own damn job. Find that other asshole."

A disturbed chief turned to go when he stopped and turned to face Carmine again as he said, "I am doing my job Carmine. You just stay out of my way."

"And if, as some of my friends have mentioned to me, if it's your son that was the accomplice, what then chief?" Carmine asked as he drew out the last word.

Galen turned quickly and stormed out of the room. As he strode down the hall he said under his breath, "Damn that boy!"

The thick colorful curtains could barely keep the intense morning sun out of the room. Sarge woke early because of the sun peeking around the curtains and looked at the pretty face lying next to him to be sure that he wasn't dreaming. Feeling Sarge staring at her, Sadie slowly opened her eyes and returned Sarge's look. He smiled. She giggled. They made love. Again.

After that Sarge jumped from the bed knowing for sure that he was not dreaming and ready to take on the day.

"Let's get on the beach, Sadie," Sarge said as he pulled on his swimsuit and looked around for his flip flops.

"Okay. Give me a minute to comb my hair and stuff."

It was the "and stuff" that made the antsy Sarge resign and flop back down on the bed.

"Sarge," Sadie said as she made her way into the bathroom, "You can go down to the beach and get us a couple chairs and I'll be down in a couple minutes, if you like."

Sarge jumped off the bed, grabbed her and gave her a big hug while twirling her around, then gave her a kiss on the lips and set her back down saying, "Excellent. Bring some bottled water with you. I'll go get us some chairs under a chicki."

"A what?" Sadie asked.

"A chicki, you know those umbrella things made out of a wood pole with a palm roof."

"Oh okay. A chicki."

"Yeah," Sarge said, "A chicki for my chickie!"

Sarge stretched as soon as he left the building as the bright sunshine hit him and he looked directly at the sun as if thanking Mother Nature for the beautiful weather. He strode confidently across the pool area heading towards the clean white sand and the lapping sound of the Caribbean Sea. He stopped under a chicki to survey the area and decide on the perfect spot to spend the day. After making his decision, he picked a chicki closest to the water so nothing and no one would obstruct his view, he hung his towel on the post and drug two lounge chairs over, placing one in the direct sun for Sadie, and the other in the shade of the chicki for himself. Sarge spread out on the lounge chair enjoying the early morning quiet with no sounds except that of the swaying palms and the lapping Sea. He opened the book he brought with him but his eyes would not stay focused on the words, they instantly migrated to the brilliant hues of blue in the water and how the tips of the small waves produced diamond like sparkles in the sunshine. It was as though Mother Nature were holding out her hand and rolling back her fingers in a gesture of "come here". So Sarge did, he went to the water. Cautiously getting close enough so only his toes would get wet when the small waves came into shore, and expecting the water to be quite cold. Miraculously it wasn't cold. It was quite pleasant and refreshing. Sarge threw caution to the wind and bounded into the water a few yards then diving into the calling Sea. He splashed around for a while then saw Sadie walking down the beach towards him dressed in a bright blue bikini top with a light blue flowered sarong that fluttered in the tradewinds showing off her long slim legs. Sarge ran towards her and as he was about to give her another bear hug she moved away.

"You're all wet," she squealed.

"You've got to come in," he said excitedly, "This water is so warm. It's awesome!"

"Let me put these things down and take off my sarong. Which "thingy" is ours?"

"Chicki, Babe, they are called chickis."

"Whatever."

"The one right behind you with the two lounge chairs and my towel on the back of the one chair."

Sadie hooked her towel on the chair, Hung her sarong on a rusty nail on the post of the chicki, and placed her bag with the bottled waters and books on her chair to hold down the towel. Then she slowly made her way back to the Sea that Sarge had again charged back into. She made the same hesitant sampling with her toe that Sarge had, with the same surprising revelation that the water was indeed warm, so she made her way out to the smiling Sarge.

The couple played in the salty sea water splashing each other, holding on to each other, and even taking time for a few salty kisses. Eventually they went back to the chicki to dry off.

As they approached their lounge chairs the lady in the next chicki asked them, "How's the water?"

"Fabulous," Sadie said as she dried her face with her colorful beach towel.

"I guess we'll be neighbors for the day," the lady said.

"That will be nice, " Sadie responded as she made her way over to the lady and asked, "Are you from the States also?"

"Yes, we're from Richmond, Virginia."

"Good. We're from Pennsylvania."

"Oh, whereabouts in Pennsylvania?"

"Near Altoona. A little town called Ganister."

"I've been to Altoona the lady's partner said as he rose from his lounge chair." He approached Sadie with his hand out. Sadie shook his hand as the man said, "I'm Steve. This is my lovely wife Becky."

"It's nice to meet you. I'm Sadie, and this is my husband Sarge."

Sarge meandered over and shook hands with Steve.

"I'm guessing you two are newlyweds," Steve said.

"How did you know?" Sadie asked.

"Just a good guess based on the smile that Sarge here can't seem to keep off his face every time he looks at you and the fact that he can't keep his hands off you."

Sarge's face reddened as he realized he had moved behind Saide and was holding her at her waist.

"We're here on our honeymoon," Sadie said.

"Well you sure picked the perfect place," Becky responded, "This island is seductive. You can't help but be in love here."

"Are you here for the week also?" Sarge asked Steve.

"Actually we come for two weeks. One week just wasn't enough so we started coming for two."

"So you've been here before?"

"Yes, we've been coming for five or more years now."

"Is there any place in particular that we should be sure to visit while we are here?" Sarge asked.

"There are a lot of great restaurants. And if you want to do the tourist thing are all kind s of activities."

"I don't want to spend all my time sightseeing," Sarge said.

"Being newlyweds," Steve answered, "I wouldn't think you would. You'll need some beach time and some romantic walks on the beach at night, and I'm sure you'll spend some time in your room." Steve winked at Sarge.

Sarge smiled.

Becky said to Sadie, "We're going to the Lighthouse tonight for dinner. It's a great Italian restaurant and the perfect place on the island to watch the sunset. If you want to go, you can go with us. We have a rental car."

"That's really sweet of you to offer. We'll talk that over and let you know," Sadie said.

"We'll be right here all day," Steve said, "If you need anything just yell."

"It was really nice meeting you folks," Sarge said as he again shook Steve's hand then he and Sadie walked the couple steps back to their chicki.

Amy had made an appointment so they were met at the door when they arrived at NCIS.

"Mr. Morrow," the young lady said, "I'll take you to the investigator's office if you two will follow me?"

The investigator was waiting and wasted no time in laying out all the evidence they had produced from the investigation.

"Was there a push to close this case fast?" Bobby asked.

The investigator paused then responded, "I would not normally say this, but I checked you out and you have quite a reputation, so I will tell you that, yes we had some pressure from above to quickly and quietly close the case as it appeared to be a suicide."

"And so you did not examine the blood spray pattern?"

"We did that, yes, and found it to be consistent with a shot in the right temple."

"But," Bobby said, "The Colonel was left-handed."

The investigator drew his left hand up to his left temple and a furrow developed on his forehead. Most people were right-handed. The Colonel was assumed to be right-handed and thus the blood spray pattern was consistent with a suicide. Why would someone change hands to commit suicide?

Bobby picked up the gun that was sealed in a clear plastic bag and asked, "Is this the weapon he used?"

"Yes, sir, and his prints were the only prints on it."

"It's a Taurus."

"Yes, sir, early vintage. Made in Brazil," the investigator thought for a moment then asked Bobby, "Is that a problem?"

"I have known the Colonel for way too many years than I care to remember. The Colonel had an extensive gun collection and we spent many hours talking about guns," Bobby said, "And one thing I remember the Colonel saying was he would never own a Taurus as they were so unreliable."

"What are you saying?" the investigator asked.

"The Colonel did not commit suicide," Bobby said. Bobby then looked at Amy and said to her, "We need to go."

"Mr. Morrow," the investigator asked, "Do you have an idea who did this?"

Bobby gave the investigator a half smile and again said to Amy, "We have to go."

Sarge and Sadie spent the morning soaking up sun. Venturing into the clear blue sea every few minutes and basically lounging away the morning. They walked the few steps to the poolside bar and ordered burgers for lunch then went right back to their chicki for more sand and sun. On one of their trips back to the chicki from the water, Sadie walked over to Becky's chicki to tell her, "If you were serious, we would like to take you up on your offer to go to the Lighthouse for dinner this evening."

"That's wonderful," Becky exclaimed.

"When do you want us to be ready?"

"We should go about 6:30 so we are there in time for the sunset."

"Perfect."

"We'll meet you in the lobby around 6:30," Becky said.

"We really appreciate you doing this for us."

"You are going to love this restaurant. It is so romantic."

Sadie blushed as she turned to tell Sarge they needed to be in the lobby at 6:30.

"No problem," Sarge said, "But for now, we need to take our towels and things to the room and get a taxi, because we promised Captain Cayce we would take his submarine ride this afternoon."

"Oh I almost forgot," Sadie said as she gathered up her belongings.

As they were leaving, Sadie said to Becky, "We have to run. We have an appointment for a submarine ride this afternoon."

"So you met Captain Cayce?" Steve asked.

A shocked Sadie stopped in her tracks and asked, "You know Captain Cayce?"

"Sure," Becky said, "Actually we are related. He's from Richmond also."

"Wow, small world," Sarge said as they held hands and walked to their room.

The submarine ride showed Sadie and Sarge a whole different world from what they were used to. Fifty feet under the Caribbean Sea and it was clear as a bell. You could actually see what was going on at the bottom of the Sea. The water was so clean and clear that light penetrated that far down. The sight was amazing. Elkhorn coral, barrel sponges, brain coral and of course, numerous fish. Fish of every size and color motoring around the coral. Parrot fish with their beak-like mouth were scraping the coral while tangs swam by in large schools changing color from deep blue to gray as they passed by. An octopus crawled out of a crack in the brain coral that did not look any where big enough to contain the eight legged brown ball. When the tour ended and they were leaving the submarine Captain Cayce approached the couple, "Thank you for taking time to enjoy our underwater world."

"We wouldn't have missed it for the world," Sadie said.

"You are too kind," the Captain said, "But I know how busy you newlyweds are and so I'm quite pleased that you chose to spend some time doing this."

Sadie gave the Captain a peck on the cheek as they left.

"He is such a nice man," Sadie said to Sarge.

"Yes he is," Sarge agreed, "We have only been here a day and we have already met several really nice people."

"Yes, and they are from the States."

"True, but the people at the Aruba Beach Club have been extremely nice also and they live here."

"Yes the Aruban people are unbelievably sweet and gracious."

"We better catch a cab and get back so we can get ready for our dinner this evening. We don't want to miss our ride."

Sadie was dressed in a light blue sundress with tropical flowers on it while Sarge had changed into tropical khaki pants and a red flowered shirt reminiscent of Magnum PI. When they met up with the Hughes in the lobby, Steve also had on khaki pants and a floral shirt while Becky looked stunning showing off her tan in a short white sundress with just a simple gold necklace glistening around her neck. When they arrived at the lighthouse, the Aruban waiter was dressed in his tuxedo and carried the large leather bound menus in the crook of his folded arm as he led the couples to a table for two down on the outdoor patio. After everyone was seated the waiter handed out the menus and the wine menu, advised the patrons of the catch of the day, and took their drink order. The couples talked but were all aware of the large bright ball of sun as it made its way across the sky to take its turn at swimming in the glistening Caribbean Sea. When the last remnants of the sun were still visible the patio came alive with cameras and cell phones all attempting to capture the final orange glow of the sun in perpetuity. The stars twinkled above, the candles on the tables began to glow and the waiters started serving the delicious Italian dishes that were the second reason why tourists flocked to this restaurant. With full bellies the foursome made the short drive down the coast past the high rise hotels to the low rise area where their rooms would welcome them for a night's sleep.

The sun poked its long yellow tendrils through Sarge's curtain again the next morning. And after consummating their marriage for the umpteenth time in just a few days, Sarge meandered to the beach to save what had now become his favorite chicki. Becky and Steve had arrived earlier to their favorite chicki and the couples became beach neighbors again.
"Thank you again for taking us to the Lighthouse last night," Sarge said.
"You are quite welcome," Becky said, "We enjoyed it also."
"Where's your bride?" Steve asked.
"She's doing those primping things that take up way too much beach time."
"What are you two planning to do today?" Becky asked.
"I think we are going to spend the whole day here on the beach," Sarge replied.
"You can't go wrong with that," Steve added.
"Tonight we may just walk over to Pizza Bob's. I get withdrawal angst if I don't have my pizza regular," said Sarge.
"You sound just like Steve," Becky said.
Steve rolled his eyes then said, "A man's got to have his pizza."
Sadie arrived showing off a new bikini and sarong and joined the conversation for a few minutes then Sarge grabbed her and carried her to the water. They frolicked in the water for a few minutes before walking back hand in hand to the waiting lounge chairs where they dried off and settled in to catch some rays from the glorious orb overhead.
Sarge was trying to read a new Jack Reacher novel but his eyelids were closed most of the time. Sadie asked him if he

wanted to go back in the water but when he didn't answer and she saw the book covering his face, she decided to go alone. Sadie took her time going out into the Sea and after she was out as far as she cared to go she bumped her toe on a large orange colored starfish. She stood still watching it for a few minutes but it did what starfish did, it just laid in the sand.

Sarge had awakened from his reading and noticing that Sadie was not on her lounge chair began scanning the water.

Steve said to Sarge, "I hate that those jetskis come down here and keep me awake with all their noise."

"Where do they come from?" Sarge inquired as he watched them come down the coast.

"Up at the high rise area," Steve said.

"Yes, they have every toy imaginable up there to rent," Becky said, "That's one more reason why we stay in this area."

"They sure get awfully close to the shore, don't they?" Sarge said.

"Yes, I'm sure somebody will get hurt one of these days." The words were no sooner out of Steve's mouth when the jetski turned in extremely close to Sadie. The man on the back of the jetski reached out and grabbed Sadie by the arms pulling her onto the jetski as the driver made a sharp right turn and sped back up the coast. Sarge was off the lounge chair running full speed up the sandy beach with no hope of ever catching the speeding jetski as Sadie's words echoed off the water, "Sarge, help me!"

Sarge ran back to the chicki where Becky said to him, "Steve has gone to the room to get the car keys. He said for you to meet him out front."

Sarge ran to the lobby not bothering to put on his flip flops or even a shirt. The anger grew inside him and if he caught these two punks he was prepared to go off on them like the worst volcano they could ever imagine. Nobody harmed Sarge's new bride. Nobody.

Steve ran out the front entrance and motioned for Sarge to follow him. They ran to the car, jumped in and sped out of the parking lot onto the highway that ran up the coast. Sarge kept his eyes peeled to the water as Steve drove as fast as he could, passing every car on the highway and only slowing for the couple of stoplights they encountered. When they got to the high rise area, they still had not seen any sign of the jetski. Suddenly Steve made a sharp left turn and headed for the beach.

"Do you see them?" Sarge asked.

"No, but I see the booth where they rent jetskis. Let's check there."

Steve haphazardly parked the car and the two men ran to the booth. Sarge pushed a young couple out of the way and began questioning the attendant. The attendant smiled as Sarge babbled on until Sarge had enough and leapt over the counter where he grabbed the attendant around the throat shoving him up against the wall.

"Now what the hell do you think is so funny?" Sarge demanded.

"Nothing funny," the attendant tried to get out of his closing airway, "But man said you would be angry. He also said you would not harm me."

"What man?"

"Man that paid me to rent jetski then came back with blonde girl. He said he playing joke on you."

"I'm going to give him joke alright. Where is this man? Who is he?"

"I don't know his name. He come and pay extra, then he leave this envelope for you."

"Give me the envelope. What's taking you so long?" Sarge growled.

Sarge let go of the man's neck and he went back to the counter where he picked up an envelope that he handed to Sarge.

Sarge tore the envelope open and read it. Steve stood watching but after a moment asked, "What's it say Sarge?" Sarge being a man of few words handed the note to Steve while he asked the attendant, "Do you have a telephone?"

"No have telephone."

"Where is the nearest one?"

The attendant pointed to the Marriott.

Steve read the note: *Call your dense friend Bobby and tell him I left him enough clues. He is to come to me, otherwise I will be keeping your wife. If you call him immediately she will be back at the Aruba Beach Club when you get there. If Morrow fails to show, I will come back for her. Signed, Derrell Sherrod*

Steve looked up from the note but Sarge was already running for the Marriott.

Steve waited near the car but it wasn't long before Sarge was piling into the passenger seat.

"What do you want me to do?" Steve asked.

"Let's go back to the resort and see if she is there, if she's not then maybe you can take me to the police station."

"Sure," Steve said as he started the little rental car and aimed it back down the coast, "Can I ask you something Sarge?"

"Sure, what would you like to know?"

"Exactly what line of work are you in? And who is Morrow?"

Sarge looked over at Steve and answered him, "I used to be a federal undercover agent. Bobby Morrow trained me and I worked for him."

"So who is the guy that signed the note?"

"I don't know. That was before my time. It was a case that Bobby worked on."

"Were you able to call Morrow?"

"Yes. He was just on his way home from Washington, DC, where he was at the funeral of his friend and our former employer, the Colonel."

"What's the Colonel's name?"

"Just the Colonel. You would remember him from the Vietnam war where he was in command then he became the confidential advisor to several presidents."

"That Colonel? Everyone knows about him. You worked for him?"

"Yes."

Steve and Sarge arrived at the resort and they both loped down to the beach after checking for Sadie in the lobby. When they got to the chickis, Sadie and Becky were in a very animated conversation.

"Sadie was just telling me how those guys took her up the coast then put her in a car and brought her right back down," Becky said to Steve and Sarge.

"Did they hurt you?" Sarge asked Sadie.

"No. Other then rubbed my arm a little when they pulled me onto that stupid jetski," Sadie answered. Then continued, "What is this all about Sarge?"

"Apparently one of Bobby's past cases is trying to get him to go to Venezuela."

"What does that have to do with us? And how do they know you and me? And how do they know we are here?"

"The scum of the world have no problem keeping track of other people and they would have done their research to find out that Bobby and I worked together. Since our marriage was just in the newspaper, they probably found that on the internet also."

"Are we safe?"

"Yes, we're safe or they would not have let you go. Bobby is not safe though. They obviously are luring him to Venezuela for some kind of revenge or something."

Sarge looked to Steve and asked, "Do you still have the note?"

"Sure," he said as he pulled it from his pocket and handed it to Sarge. Sarge tucked the note inside his book.

"Take me back to the Colonel's office," Bobby said to Amy, "I have to get my car and head back home.

Bobby's cell phone rang and he answered it, "Sarge what are you calling me for? Aren't you on your honeymoon?"

"Yes, but I just had an incident."

"What kind of incident?"

"Sadie and I were on the beach. I fell asleep in the lounge chair and she went out into the water. Some guys came by on a jetski and snatched her…"

"Did you get her back? Is she alright?"

"Yes they brought her back on the condition that I phone you immediately and give you a message."

"What's the message?"

"They said they have given you enough clues. You are now to go meet a Derrell Sherrod."

Bobby was silent for a moment so Sarge asked, "Bobby who is Derrell Sherrod?"

"He's Cordell Sherrod's brother."

"And so who is Cordell Sherrod?"

"Before you came along, there was an undercover agent in Bonaire, only two islands away from where you are now. His name was Wildman Clint Armstrong. He was ready to nail Cordell for running drugs from Venezuela to Bonaire then onto Europe and the U.S.. Sherrod killed Armstrong. I caught Sherrod with Richard's help and he got sent to Guantanamo Bay where I believe he still is."

"And so Derrell wants revenge?"

"No doubt. After all his brother is rotting in a cell in Guantanamo."

"Bobby you can't go there alone," Sarge pleaded.

"I have to. They will know if anyone else is with me or in the background lurking."

"But you know they are going to kill you."

"You're probably right about that. Unless I can get them first."

"I'm just across the Caribbean from them. I'll meet you there."
"You will not! That is an order. You will finish your honeymoon and you will go home. I got this covered," Bobby said.
"That's what you said last Thanksgiving when you decided to not have your wife do all the cooking and you deep fried the turkey. You damn near burnt down your house."
"But I didn't. And I've done this before. That was my first time cooking a turkey. Who knew it would spit all that hot oil everywhere when you dropped the turkey in?"
"You weren't supposed to drop the turkey in. The directions specifically said, slowly place the turkey in the hot grease."
"I was in a hurry."
"Like you are now?"
Bobby ended the call then placed another call.
"Amy, I have to go to Venezuela."
"Does this have anything to do with the Colonel?" she asked.
"Yes. And it solves his murder. Derrell Sherrod, brother of Cordell Sherrod that we put away, the Colonel and I, has just contacted me through Sarge. He said he has left me enough clues, which would be the Taurus gun that the Colonel supposedly shot himself with. The Taurus was Sherrod's gun of choice and the Colonel would never own one. They shot the Colonel in the head from the right side knowing that the Colonel was left handed. Apparently they intend to take care of everyone that had anything to do with putting Cordell away. And I'm next on the list."
"You can't go there alone."
"I have to."

Chapter 9

Soaking up sunshine and playing in the Caribbean Sea was hard work and when the sun went down Sadie was ready for bed. She slept soundly while Sarge tossed and turned. After a while he thought he better get up before he woke Sadie so he pulled on some clothes and made his way down to the beach bar where Jimmy Buffet music was playing away while the bartender passed out cold beers and colorful drinks with umbrellas in them. Sarge found an open seat and with a slight motion to the bartender was quickly drinking a Bright beer. After all, while in Aruba, drink what the Arubans drink. Sarge was deep in thought as he fretted over what may happen to Bobby and how bad the timing was. If only he hadn't just got married, he could assist Bobby.

A quick slap on Sarge's broad shoulder made him jump.

"Sarge, what are you doing here? Don't you have a lovely new wife to snuggle up next to?"

"That I do Captain Cayce," Sarge said with a slight smile on his face.

"So what's the problem?"

"Not really anything I can discuss Captain," Sarge replied.

"Well you look like your favorite pet died."

Sarge studied a minute then answered, "That might be fairly accurate."

"Then allow me to help you," Captain Cayce said. "But first buy me a drink."

Cayce motioned for the bartender who without asking brought the Captain a shot and set it in front of him. Cayce tipped the shotglass up and after swiping his mouth with his hand said, "Sm-o-o-oth!", drawing the word out into a short sentence.

"I'm afraid there isn't anything you can do to help Captain. But I appreciate the thought."

The Captain pulled himself onto the high barstool and with a smirk on his face said to Sarge, "You may be surprised at what I can do?"

Sarge took a gulp of beer, "Like what? You want to lend me your submarine?"

Cayce slapped Sarge on the shoulder again, "That submarine's just for tourists, that thing wouldn't do you any good."

"Well the only way you could help me Captain is to smuggle me onto the beach in Venezuela and provide me with a map to the local druglord's lair," Sarge said as he took another gulp of beer and continued, "This isn't bad beer."

"It's the water."

"What?" Sarge asked shaking off the fog that was settling around his brain from the beer.

"It's the water. Aruba makes all of their own water from sea water so it's great water which makes good beer."

"Oh, I see."

"And I could get you onto the beach," the Captain said quietly, "And I can probably even get you a map to Sherrod's. I assume that's the druglord you are talking about?"

The fog disappeared from Sarge's brain as he concentrated on what he thought he had just heard the Captain say then he asked, "Did you just say…"

The Captain put his finger to his lips as a sign for Sarge to not speak. Sarge looked around then stared at Cayce and quietly asked, "Captain, who are you really?"

Cayce smiled and began singing, "Do, dat, da, diddy, de…"

"Captain?" Sarge asked again.

"Let's take a walk on the beach," Cayce said. "Not like you and your new bride would, but close enough to the water that only you and God can hear me."

Sarge motioned for the bartender and threw some money on the bar as he stood to leave. More money than was necessary including a handsome tip. The bartender smiled and said to Sarge as he was walking away with the Captain, "You come back now."

Neither spoke until they reached the water's edge where the surf was lapping onto the packed sand providing pleasant background music.

"I heard of Sherrod before I retired," the Captain said.

"Exactly what did you retire from?" Sarge asked.

"Government work," Cayce said meaning for that to be the end of that particular conversation.

"Someplace with Initials and not a name, I assume."

"Anyway," the Captain said as he pointed out into the dark Sea, "17 miles that direction, or 14.7 nautical miles, is the coast of Venezuela. Sherrod's compound is on the west side of the cape, north of the town of Punta Fijo, and it's situated along the coast."

"Then all we need is a boat," Sarge said.

Cayce held up his hand to stop Sarge, "It's not that easy. They have regular patrols along the coast plus they have a manned tower that scours the water for boats. A boat could not get near that place."

"Then how can I get there?"

"Have you ever heard of the Super Falcon?" the Captain asked.

Sarge shook his head negatively.

"The Super Falcon, is a two man, winged submersible made by Hawkes Ocean Technologies."

"I don't mean to be a wet blanket Captain," Sarge said, "But I'm rather sure I can't drive a submersible and if you go along that makes three people after we collect Bobby."

"I said they make a two man submersible. The one I have access to is slightly modified, it will hold three people. We've used it on a few occasions to take Navy Seals over to Colombia."

"We?" Sarge asked hoping to find out a bit more about the Captain.

"I'm a Captain. I drive boats and subs or anything that goes into the water."

"Bobby will be there tomorrow morning," Sarge stated.

"We will have no choice but to wait until nightfall to go in after him. I'll pick you up outside the lobby tomorrow night about one o'clock a.m., and that will put us there around two in the morning when they should start getting lackadaisical. But you have to realize, I'm a lover not a fighter. I'll get you there and I'll get you back but it will be up to you to spring your Mr. Morrow."

"I hope he's not dead by then or too badly beaten."

"I'm afraid it's the best we can do."

"He is a tough guy so we'll assume he'll still have all his body parts intact and can walk out of the compound. You wouldn't happen to have a map of the compound would you?"

The Captain snickered, "What do you think I am, a travel agent? No, I don't have a map but I will bring along a little something that will help you."

"What's that?"

"Night vision binoculars with heat imaging recognition. You will at least be able to tell where the bodies are located."

"That will be fabulous," Sarge said, "I suppose I shouldn't ask how you happen to have them?"

"It's probably best you don't ask. But let me ask you, Is your major medical insurance paid up? Because you are walking into a regular viper's nest."

"He's my friend," Sarge said, "There is nothing I wouldn't do to help Bobby. Nothing!"

The finality of Sarge's statement left no doubt in Cayce's mind that Sarge was a warrior and true to his word. Nothing would stop him.

The Captain turned and walked away singing, "Tomorrow. Dum, da dee, da, doo, …scooby dooby doo….."

Sarge was able to quietly reenter his room and slide under the covers next to his beautiful bride without waking her. When sleep finally came to him, it was quickly chased away by intruding rays of glorious sunshine. Sarge looked over at Sadie. Sadie smiled back at him.

While Sarge and Sadie were frolicking between the sheets, then soaking up sunshine while occasionally cooling their bodies with salt water, Bobby Morrow willingly stepped off an airplane, went through Venezuelan Customs and was met at the airport entrance by several of the meanest looking men in South America. They gruffly grabbed Bobby, one man on each side, and practically drug him across the concrete into a waiting car with blacked-out windows. After roughly throwing him into the backseat another ruffian began to search him.

"I just got off an airplane," Bobby said, "exactly where the hell do you think I would be able to conceal a weapon? Have you been through airport security in the United States lately? Hell, they wouldn't even allow me to bring my toenail clippers so I could give you a pedicure."

"Shut up Gringo," one of the men said in broken english, "You talk too much."

"You think this is bad, you should see my daughter."

The ruffian next to Bobby slapped duct tape over Bobby's mouth then grabbed his wrists and bound them with a plastic zip-tie as tightly as he could.

Bobby saved his energy. The car ride was not very long and under different circumstances the scenery would have been very pleasing. Especially when they drove out onto the neck of the cape where you could see the shimmering blue Caribbean Sea on both sides of the highway. Shortly after that they passed through the rusty metal gates of a compound which was overloaded with shirtless men bearing guns of all sizes and shapes. The ruffian pulled Bobby out of the backseat as soon as the car slid to a stop and held him up while Derrell Sherrod strode up like a four star general. Sherrod punched Bobby in the stomach as hard as he could while two men firmly held onto Bobby's arms. Bobby spat something out which was indecipherable due to the duct tape on his mouth. Derrell reached over and roughly pulled the duct tape from Bobby's mouth, "Did you say something Mr. Morrow?"

"I merely asked if that was your best punch. You hit like a girl," Bobby said with a snicker on his face.

Immediately another punch struck Bobby in the gut.

"How about you tell the goons to go away then you and I can get to it?" Bobby asked Derrell.

"You insist on being a tough guy," Derrell said, "Well we're going to take some of the tough out of you." Derrell placed a finger in front of his mouth while holding up his arm with the other arm then said, "Correction, we are going to take *all* of the tough out of you. Every last breath."

"I hope you packed a lunch Derrell because if you're doing the beating it's going to be a long day."

"Take that piece of gringo dung into the shed and string him up. I'll be there after I have a nice leisurely lunch. It's hot, perhaps I'll also have a nice mojito."

"Have one of your goons bring a mojito out to me," Bobby

shouted to Derrell as they carried him off with his feet dragging in the red dirt causing dust to fly into the air. Derrell Sherrod entered the building where Bobby hung, patting his stomach after his delicious lunch of conch salad and mojitos, and carrying an electric cattle prod.

"Not getting enough, you have to use an artificial stimulator?" Bobby asked.

"I intend to stimulate you, my friend," said a calm Sherrod.

"Then you better hope I don't get loose Sherrod because if I do the first item on my agenda will be to stick that cattle prod where the sun don't shine."

"We'll see how tough you are in a minute," Sherrod said with a smile on his face.

Sherrod took his time rolling up the sleeves of his fine silk shirt then admired the cattle prod and watching the sparks fly as he pressed the button for show. Slowly he advanced towards Bobby with the cattle prod held out in front of himself.

It was extremely easy for Sarge to fall asleep under the chicki. All comfortable on the lounge chair and with the intention of reading a few more chapters of the Jack Reacher book but with the long night talking with Captain Cayce and worrying about Bobby sleep was only now advancing upon him. Sadie would get up from her sun worshipping every now and then to ask Sarge if he wanted to join her in the deep blue Sea, but each time her request was met with snores coming from under the book covering Sarge's face, so she went in alone to enjoy the water on her hot tanned body. Sarge did awake around lunchtime and said to Sadie, "Wow, I must have fell asleep, do you want to get something to eat?"

"Sure, what did you have in mind?"

"I think I'd like a fresh Wahoo sandwich from the beach bar," Sarge said.

"That sounds good," answered Sadie. "Do you want me to go get them?"

"I'll go," Sarge said, "I need the exercise."

"I thought maybe I was wearing you out," Sadie said as she smiled up at Sarge.

Sarge was at a loss for words so he put down his book, rounded up his plastic sandwich bag with his cash and credit cards in it, or as it is called here on the island, his Aruban wallet, slipped into his flip flops and headed for the beach bar. After lunch a few more exhausting hours of playing in the sun, sand, and sea, plus chatting with their chicki neighbors, the couple decided to go to their room and shower for dinner. As the couple passed their chicki neighbors, Sarge stopped to quietly speak with Steve.

"Will you please check on Sadie in the morning? We are in room 219," Sarge asked Steve.

"Sure. Of course," Steve said with concern emanating from his face, "Is anything wrong?"

"I have to go somewhere late tonight and I just need to know that someone will look after her," Sarge said as he handed Steve a folded piece of paper. "Here are some numbers in case there are any problems. Please contact her father and the other number."

Steve looked at the paper as he responded, "Is there anything else I can do?"

"Thanks, but no."

"Is this about the note you received the other day when the jetskiers snatched Sadie?"

"Yes, but you will be better off not knowing too much."

"I looked that Sherrod name up on the internet last night," Steve said, "I saw that there are drug dealers in Venezuela by that name."

"You should forget that you know that," Sarge advised Steve.

Steve stared at Sarge for a few moments before saying, "You're going there aren't you?"

Sarge turned to walk away when Steve grabbed Sarge's beefy arm to stop him and asked, "Can I go with you?"

"I need you here," Sarge said as he walked away to catch up with Sadie who was standing at the edge of the patio using the outdoor shower to wash the sand off her feet before putting on her flip flops.

Becky was good at reading body language and immediately asked Steve, "What's going on Steve?"

"We need to keep an eye on Sadie. There's a storm brewing in the Caribbean."

Sarge hailed a taxi in front of the resort and he and Sadie climbed in the backseat.

"Where to?" the taxi driver asked.

"Iguana Moe's" Sarge replied.

"Very good," said the taxi driver as he checked his mirrors and pulled out from the resort. They arrived in just a few minutes and after Sarge paid the taxi driver the couple walked up the steps to the second floor restaurant that overlooked the downtown area and the cruise ships that were in the harbor. The waitress seated the couple, brought menus, and asked for their drink order.

"Cactus colada for me," said Sarge. "What would you like Sadie?"

"I'll try the same thing. No, on second thought, I want a Mango daiquiri."

"I'll be back in a minute with your drinks," said the waitress as she left the table.

The ambience of the open air restaurant with the cruise ships anchored on the shimmering blue sea and the trade winds carrying the smells of exotic plants and whatever was cooking in the kitchen was exciting. The waitress returned with their drinks and took their food order. The couple clinked glasses as the couple said in unison, "You and me. May we always be - Together!"

Sarge put his hand on top of Sadie's and told her he loved her.

When they returned to the Aruba Beach Club, Sarge let out a yawn while stretching his muscular arms up in the air. "I think we should go to bed early tonight," he said. And they did.

Sarge woke after midnight and quietly moved out of the bed, pulled on some black clothes and snuck out of the room while Sadie slept peacefully. The Captain, being a man of his word, was waiting in his car in front of the resort with the motor running. Sarge jumped in and the vehicle sped off. When they reached the Captain's office they climbed on board a small boat. Sarge looked questioningly at the Captain but he merely motored the boat out of the slip and headed for the dark Sea. When the Captain passed the outer small islands that ring the downtown harbor he made a sharp left turn and sped along the coast past the airport and the brewery which were both lit up like a ball park on the night of a big game. Cayce slowed as he came upon an old steel sided shed that jutted out into the water. He pulled up next to the connected dock and turned off the boat motor, motioned to Sarge to follow him and he jumped from the boat with a rope in his hand to tie up the motor boat. After a quick glance around Cayce put a key into the lock on the steel covered door and entered the shed. He motioned for Sarge to follow into the darkness as he again glanced around the perimeter. After Sarge was inside Cayce closed the door and turned on the lights. The Super Falcon looked to Sarge like something out of a James Bond movie, it was a submersible, or maybe an airplane, or possibly a mixture of both. It had three round glass tops lined up on the slender body which also had short wings on the sides. Sarge stared in amazement.

"She's a beauty, isn't she?" Cayce asked.

"Are you sure this thing will hold three of us?" Sarge asked.

"Of course," Cayce said as he began to lower the custom built submersible into the water. The glass hatches opened when Cayce pushed a remote and he said to Sarge, "You sit in the middle hatch." Sarge gingerly stepped off the interior dock and into the open cockpit while clinging tightly to the sides as it rocked slightly on the water.

Captain Cayce then climbed into the front cockpit and closed the glass hatches. Sarge experienced a moment of anxiety then he heard Cayce's voice over an intercom, "It's just like being in an airplane except this one flies under the water. It is very safe because it is positively buoyant…."

Sarge interrupted, "What the hell does that mean?"

Cayce answered with a laugh in his voice, "It means that it remains floating unless some mechanical device or additional weight is used. In other words we force it under water the same way a whale would dive or you would dive under water. Saying that, the captain massaged the controls and said to Sarge, "Here we go."

Sarge hung on tight to the seat rails as he watched the water rise up and over the glass hatch. In a matter of seconds he was under water. Under the dark black water where the only thing he could see was what was lit up by the bright lights on the front of the craft. By the time they reached their stopping point Sarge had relaxed and was almost enjoying the sights of the underwater nightlife where the octopus, shrimp, lobster, and other marine life came out to feed. Cayce raised the submersible so that only the three glass hatches were above the water line then he said to Sarge, "When I open the hatch grab the waterproof bag at your feet and jump out quick. I can't stay here long or eventually they will spot us. Remember the spot on the beach where you go ashore and when you come back just swim out a few yards. I'll be waiting." The hatch opened, Sarge grabbed the black waterproof bag and jumped over the side into the refreshing sea water and swam towards shore. He looked back after a minute but there was nothing to see. The captain and his craft were gone. Sarge crawled onto the beach on his belly dragging the bag for a few yards then jumped up and sprinted into the palm trees on the

other side of the beach where he immediately took cover and listened for any sounds that he may have alerted someone. He then opened the bag to see what Cayce had given him. Two Glock pistols and a Ka-bar knife along with the night vision that he had told Sarge about. Sarge stuck the knife in his waistband, and checked the clips on both Glocks. Full clips. "Thanks Captain," Sarge said under his breath, "You're a life saver."
Sarge placed the night vision on his head then like an Indian watching each footfall he headed out in the direction of the compound. At the edge of the compound Sarge scanned each of the buildings with the heat imaging feature of the night vision goggles. Several of the buildings showed bodies in a horizontal position. People sleeping. In the far building he saw a deformed body that appeared to be standing but not quite so and it was giving off large amounts of heat. Plus there were two people outside the building walking back and forth. Sarge was sure that would be where Bobby was and he moved in that direction. When he got close he quietly approached the building from the side. He waited a few minutes and eventually a guard with an assault rifle came to the edge of the building to look down the side. The guard never saw the flick of the Ka-bar as it sliced his throat open. Sarge grabbed the body before it fell over and pulled it around the side of the building then he took the assault rifle, bent over to appear smaller and walked quickly across the front of the building to the other guard. The other guard was walking straight at him and was about to question his strange appearance when the Ka-Bar knife flew through the air with tremendous speed and accuracy and sank into his chest cavity. The man reached for his chest while blood poured out from between his fingers as

he slowly sank to the ground. Sarge wasted no time entering the building where he stopped to get a good look around him before he moved on. The night vision showed a weary, bloody Bobby hanging from his arms in the center of the room. Sarge ran to him and untied the ropes that held him up.

"Are you going to make it?" Sarge asked Bobby.

"I was saving my strength so I could open a can of whip-ass on these guys in the morning."

"Sure you were," said Sarge. "How about we get the hell out of here?"

"Let me get my legs under me first," Bobby said. "Then I have to have a word with Sherrod. It wouldn't be polite to leave without expressing my gratitude for his hospitality."

"Or we could just get out of here!"

"It will only take a second. He's in the next building, probably sleeping."

"Then we should let him sleep," Sarge said to Bobby's back as Bobby walked unsteadily to the door. Sarge followed and when they went out the door, Sarge scanned the area with the night vision checking for more guards. Bobby picked up his pace as he went to the next building where he strode up to the door, turned the knob and strolled in making his way through the house until he came to the bedroom. He opened the bedroom door and walked up to the side of the bed. Derrell was sound asleep with his arm around a slender long haired female. Bobby slapped Derrell lightly across the face. Derrell awoke and panic swept over his face.

"I didn't want to leave without thanking you for your hospitality," Bobby said as Derrell tried to slide up the bed away from Bobby. "I especially enjoyed the shock therapy. I was sort of in a funk and that put new spark in my life. And the beatings reminded me that I may have let myself go a little so I'm going to get back to the gym when I get home and get in shape."

Derrell lunged for the nightstand pulling open the drawer and reaching for a gun. Bobby grabbed his hand with the gun in it and summoning his testosterone he overpowered Derrell. Bobby placed the gun against Derrell's head then asked him, "Is this how you shot the Colonel?"

Derrell spit at Bobby. Bobby pulled the trigger. The frightened woman that had been lying next to Derrell was now screaming.

Bobby tried to comfort her, "One day you'll thank me for this."

"Can we go now?" Sarge asked.

Bobby turned and said, "Maybe you better lead the way. I had a chauffeur when I arrived."

Sarge scanned the exterior then led Bobby out of the compound the same way he entered. When they reached the beach before they left the shelter of the palms, Bobby whispered, "I assume you have a plan big guy?"

"Sure, when you're ready we are going to swim out into sea."

"I'm not sure I have the strength to swim to Aruba," Bobby said.

"It's only seventeen miles. You must be getting soft in your old age."

Bobby punched Sarge in the shoulder.

"Trust me," Sarge said.

Sarge found the waterproof bag, placed the guns and night vision equipment back in it, took one last look around and ran across the sand into the water with Bobby right on his heels. Sarge dove into the water and began swimming so Bobby followed. A few yards from shore the glass hatches arose out of the water a mere couple feet in front of the swimmers. The hatches opened, Sarge jumped into the center one and motioned for Bobby to get in the last one. Bullets started whizzing past their heads. The glass hatches closed and the submersible sank under the water. As the submersible turned away the bullets zipped past the submersible under water leaving trails.

"Welcome aboard, mates," Cayce said over the intercom.

"Captain Cayce," Bobby said excitedly, "Is that you?"

"Aye, it's me," Cayce said, "I see you are still having a problem staying out of trouble?"

"It seems to follow me Captain."

"You know you owe me a drink when we get back to Aruba."

"It will be a pleasure to buy you a drink Captain," Bobby said.

"You still drink that hundred and fifty proof rum?"

"Good memory."

Sarge interjected, "You mean you two know each other?"

"Sarge how long have you known Bobby?" Cayce asked.

"For a few years now."

"Then you should know that someone has to be available to pull his butt out of the predicaments he gets into."

"I should have guessed. Maybe you can tell me some stories when we get back Captain."

"Oh, I could, but, as they say, then I'd have to kill you."

The submersible pulled into the old steel shack and rose above the water level. The hatches opened and the trio jumped out of the submersible onto the interior dock. The Captain pushed the remote and the submersible was raised above the water.

"Sarge, we better get you back before your bride misses you and Bobby you can stay at my place tonight since your flight doesn't leave until tomorrow," the Captain stated as he led them out of the old steel shed and locked the door.

Sarge quietly entered the room, undressed and slipped under the covers.

"You're not going to make a habit of this are you?" Sadie whipered.

"No dear. Please go back to sleep."

"I will but first......"

Chapter 10

Sarge was not only prepared for the early morning sunshine to penetrate his room, he was welcoming it. He kissed his bride, got the towels, books, and sunscreen and said to Sadie, "I'll get us a chicki. Then I'll meet you at the beach restaurant for breakfast."

"Sounds good to me," Sadie answered.

Sarge strode through the sand to his favorite chicki and spread the towels on the lounge chairs then went back to the restaurant at the edge of the sand. He picked a table at the edge of the sand where he could watch the calm blue sea and waited for Sadie. The Hughes came into the restaurant and Sarge motioned for them to join him.

"Sarge," an elated Steve said, "I'm glad to see you. How was your evening?"

Sarge nodded his head while saying, "It was good."

Becky looked at Steve feeling left out of the conversation and asked Steve, "I thought you said there was a storm brewing, look at this beautiful day."

Steve winked at Sarge and said, "Apparently the storm has passed Becky."

Sadie came in showing off another new bikini and sarong as the waitress appeared with the menus and water. The couples ordered breakfast when from behind Sarge a voice said, "Do you like that as well as what they are wearing this year?" Sarge turned and smiled, "What, Captain, you don't like my flowered shirt?"

"It's fine," Cayce said, "Did it come with a whistle?"

"Please join us, Captain," Sadie said. "I believe you already know Steve and Becky? Sarge you may need to introduce Bobby to the Hughes."

Sarge made the introductions as he and Steve pulled another table over to theirs to make room for everyone.

"Bobby," Sadie asked, "Where did you take my husband last night?"

Bobby looked at Sarge who shrugged his shoulders.

Cayce interjected, "I'm afraid that was my fault, dear, I took them on a late night boat ride. Some of the marine life only comes out at night and I wanted them to see it."

"I wish I could have gone," Steve said.

"The next time you come to Aruba, Steve, you and I will go out at night," Cayce said, "If that's alright with Becky."

"Steve can go," Becky said, "But you're not getting me out there in the dark on a boat."

Sarge elbowed Bobby and then pointed, "There's that beautiful woman that was at Richard St.Clair's funeral."

"Nanita," Bobby shouted to her as he stood from the table. Everyone turned to see who Bobby was talking to.

"She is pretty," Sadie said. "Who is she?"

Captain Cayce eyed her up and down and said, "She doesn't affect me,….doesn't affect me,….doesn't affect me." Leaving no doubt that he was affected by her beauty.

Sarge said to Cayce, "She is beautiful, but maybe too young for you."

Cayce said to Bobby's back in his best Australian accent, "Give her a go mate, she's eighteen." With the eighteen coming out more like a-deen.

Everyone at the table laughed until tears formed in their eyes. "Where do you get this stuff?" Sarge asked Cayce.

"Back in the big war, when we got off the ship in Australia, that was what we heard a lot of: give her a go mate she's eighteen."

Sarge then looked to Sadie and told her, "To answer your question, she is the manager here and apparently she knew Senator St.Clair very well."

Nanita said to Bobby, "I had no idea that you were here, but I just received a message for Sarge and it mentioned your name. Which one is Sarge," she asked the group.

"I am," said Sarge as he stood up and Nanita handed him the message. Sarge read it then handed it to Bobby.

Bobby read the message to himself, "Sarge, if you can locate Bobby Morrow, please have him call Attorney General Ellwood Sine at his earliest convenience. His cell phone appears to be out of order."

It's more than out of order Bobby thought to himself, Derrell Sherrod's men took it and he will never get it back. Then Bobby addressed the group at the table, "Excuse me please I have to make a phone call. Nanita, do you have a telephone that I can use?"

"Of course Bobby," she said, "Please come with me." She intertwined her arm around Bobby's and they walked to her office where she had him sit at her desk and instructed him on how to reach the United States.

"Ellwood," Bobby said when the Attorney General came on the line. "What's up?"

"I've been trying to locate you. Where are you?"

"I'm in Aruba at the moment but will be taking a flight home in a couple hours."

"Dare I ask what you are doing in Aruba?"

"You probably don't want to know Ellwood," Bobby said.

"I'll just assume that it had something to do with the Colonel's death and the fact that we received word that Derrell Sherrod is dead."

Bobby did not say anything. Sometimes the unsaid speaks volumes.

"Right," Ellwood said, "Anyway I was about to ask if you could go to Aruba to do some protective work for us. Since you are already there, would you be willing to stay a few days?"

"I guess. I will need to contact my wife."

"I have already contacted her and she said you would insist on doing this detail for us."

"Really? What detail are we talking about?"

"We have a Senator's daughter that may be a prime kidnapping candidate."

"I hope you don't mean Senator Snead's daughter," Bobby said as he looked back towards the restaurant.

"I'm afraid so. We have some intel from our feet on the ground in China that they may attempt a kidnapping to coerce the Senator to relinquish the codes to the star wars satellites."

"Will you call Claire and tell her I'll be home in a few days?"

"Of course. I also need to ask you, do you need any.... shall we say....*tools*?"

"I happen to know a man who is here at breakfast with me that has some *tools* that I can borrow," Bobby replied.

"Looks like you are back on the federal payroll Bobby."

"Looks like," he said as he hung up the telephone and hurried back to the restaurant.

"What's up?" Sarge asked him as he was sitting back down to his steaming breakfast.

"Seems my plane has been delayed," Bobby said. Then he turned to Cayce and whispered, "Can I borrow your waterproof bag of goodies?"

"Certainly Bobby," Captain Cayce said, "When we leave here I'll drive you over and you can get the bag of goodies plus you may use my car while you're here. Is there anything else I can do to assist?"

"I'm going to need a cell phone and your phone number in case I get in another sticky situation. Oh, and do you have any connections here, I need a room. Preferably close to Sarge's room."

"Do I have connections?" Cayce asked. "You know I do. I'll go get you a room key now." Cayce pushed back from the table and strutted to the front desk coming back with a key to room 217 which he passed off to Bobby."

"You do have connections," said Bobby.

Cayce winked then began singing, "doot ..da deet,.. scooby , dooby, …".

When Bobby came back to the resort after he and Cayce went for the "*tools*", Bobby got Sarge alone and handed him a neatly wrapped beach towel.

"Keep this with you Sarge," he whispered.

Sarge took the towel and guessing at its contents due to the weight of the towel asked Bobby, "Is there anything I should know?"

"Stay alert and don't allow your lovely bride away from your side."

Sarge stowed the towel with its contents in his bag with his sunscreen and book and immediately assumed his position next to Sadie.

Bobby took up residence in a chicki behind Sarge and Sadie and started working on his tan. When they gathered their belongings and departed the beach Bobby did likewise at a discreet distance. Knowing the couple was having dinner at the Old Cunuchu House, Bobby discreetly followed them there and back. And when they retired to their room Bobby finally went to his room and collapsed on the bed. Assuming any good kidnapper worth his salt would wait until the wee hours of the morning when their prey would be barely coherent, Bobby laid on the bed for a quick nap, setting the alarm clock for midnight when he would resume his babysitting.

Bobby had just fallen off to sleep when he heard a light knock on the next room's door. Bobby jumped off the bed, grabbed the Glock he had placed under his pillow, ran to the door, and slowly opened his door just enough to see who was knocking on Sarge's door. Seeing that it was Steve and Becky, Bobby closed his door and flopped back on the bed.

"Oh, hi, Steve and Becky," Sarge said as he opened the door while sticking his Glock in his waistband behind his back.

"Your friend asked us to stop by," Steve said. "And take you to our room for the night. He thought it would be much safer if anyone came for you that you weren't here."

"Sarge," Sadie asked, "What is going on?"

"I didn't want to alarm you but the call that Bobby got this morning was to ask him to stay and guard us because the Chinese might be attempting to kidnap you to coerce your father to give them the star wars satellite codes."

Becky gasped, "You're kidding me."

"I'm afraid not," Sarge said, "But don't worry. Bobby is the best." Looking to Steve, Sarge said, "That's probably not a bad idea, but we sure hate to put you two out."

"You wouldn't be putting us out," Becky said, "We have a two bedroom suite. You would have your own room. And we could play Farkle."

"Farkle?" Sadie asked, "What is Farkle?"

"It's a dice game. It's really fun."

Steve whispered to Sarge, "I would ask though that you didn't bring any guns into our room. Becky is deathly afraid of them."

"I guess we won't need one when we aren't even where we're supposed to be," Sarge said as he slipped the Glock out of his waistband and placed it in the safe in the closet along with their passports and extra money.

"We don't want anyone thinking you are moving to a different room," Steve said, "So just put your night clothes in Sadie's purse."

"Good idea," said Sadie as she stuffed her nightie into her purse.

"If you're ready, we may as well head for our room."

The Hughes room was on the first floor at the end of the resort facing the ocean.

After they entered Sadie looked out the glass sliding doors at the Sea and proclaimed, "You two have an awesome suite. I would love to wake up to this each morning!"

"Your room will be this one," Becky said as she glided across the room and opened the door.

Sarge and Becky ambled into their new room. The door shut behind them and the lights went on. Two Chinese men dressed in tan suits were each training pistols on them.

"Search him," one of them said in barely understandable English.

The other carefully patted Sarge down then did the same to Sadie. It took all of Sarge's self control to not attack the man as he put his hands on Sarge's new bride.

"You will come with us," the first man said.

"You will walk in front of us and remember any wrong move and I will shoot the woman first. You understand me big man?"

Sarge nodded his head.

"Say the words," the man persisted, "Say you understand me."

"I understand you," Sarge said through gritted teeth.

"Go. Slowly. No sudden moves!"

The couple left the bedroom they didn't have time to get acquainted with passing Steve and Becky standing close together in the living room holding each other.

The first man said to Steve and Becky, "Your free Aruba vacation is now earned. Congratulations!"

Steve and Becky lowered their heads and stared at the floor.

When Sarge and Sadie reached the door the first man said, "Wait." Then to his companion he ordered, "Check the hallway."

The other man opened the door just a crack and scanned the hallway.

"Anyone there?" the first one asked?

"Only janitor scrubbing hallway."

"Remember you two, be quiet. No sudden moves. Now, go."

Sarge and Sadie led the two men out the door and down the hallway.

The janitor never looked up at them he was engrossed in swinging the big mop back and forth across the hallway as he sang "da, doot, dadoot, diddle e dee…"

Sarge and Sadie passed the janitor as he paused and stepped aside to let them by while he stared at the fresh footprints on his just washed floor and shook his head.

When the two men were directly in front of the janitor, the mop handle came down with such speed that neither man knew what happened until it had cracked across their arms knocking their guns to the floor where they skittered across the wet tile. Sarge wasted no time when he heard the gun skittering across the floor, he turned and while he was turning he pulled the long muscular arm back then unloaded a punch that had all his weight behind it knocking the first man back down the hall on his backside. The long handle of the mop then smacked the other man on the back of his head knocking him forward. Sarge grabbed him and slammed him head first into the wall. The janitor threw a ziptie to Sarge who roughly placed it on the wrists of the man who was bleeding profusely from his skull. The janitor rolled the man on the floor over and ziptied his wrists behind him as he said to the man, "You dirtied my clean floor!" For good measure he kicked him in the leg.

Steve came running out of his room when he heard the commotion. Sarge charged towards Steve but the janitor grabbed him and held him back.

"Whoa Sarge," the janitor said, "take it easy."

"But they lured us down here to get taken by these idiots. And by the way, Captain Cayce, since when are you a janitor."

"You'd be surprised where you might find me," Cayce said. "And as for Steve and Becky, they had contacted the FBI in Virginia when they were approached by men that claimed they would kill their children if they didn't do what they were ordered to do. The FBI has been watching all their children."

Steve approached Sarge, "I'm really sorry man."

"Not your fault," said Sarge as they shook hands.

Cayce pulled out his cell phone and made a call, "Clean up on aisle three."

Several police officers immediately filled the hallway and picked up the two bound men.

"Well," said Cayce, "How about a drink. The beach bar is still open."

Steve said "No thanks. I've had all the excitement I can stand for one vacation and he sauntered back his room. Cayce looked at Sarge and Sadie.

Sadie spoke, "We'd love to Captain." She grabbed his arm and off they went with Sarge following behind.

The bartender brought Captain Cayce his usual and two blue iced drinks for the newlyweds. Captain Cayce raised his glass to the couple. The three of them touched glasses as Cayce said, "Sm-o-o-o-th! Re-e-e-al Sm-o-o-o-o-th!"

The flatscreen television behind the bar was showing a newscaster from the United States.

"This just in," the talking head said, "We are being told by a reliable source that the son of a chief of police in Ganister, Pennsylvania was found dead in a field from a single gunshot wound. It is believed the victim had been deer hunting and was probably killed by a stray bullet or another hunter mistook him for a deer. The victim was wearing the required bright orange coat and hat. We will keep you updated on this as we learn more."

Sarge shook his head when he heard the news. Bobby arrived at the bar and said, "What are you all doing here?"

"Celebrating," Cayce said, "Would you like a drink?"

"How did you know we were here?" Sarge asked Bobby.

"The commotion in the hall downstairs woke me so I checked your room and you weren't there, then as I was looking out the window I see the three of you traipsing over to the beach bar.

"Some bodyguard you are," Sarge said to Bobby. "Maybe the government should pay Cayce instead of you."

Bobby smiled and said, "The government probably does pay Cayce."

"Ahh yes," Cayce said, "I get my social security check every month. Well, I must be going. Goodbye all. And remember, Tempest fugits. Tempest fugits!"

Payment for Life
By A. Wayne Ross

Excerpt from the next exciting short story featuring Chief of Police Sis Steele who has the great looks of a model but is as tough as her last name.

Chapter 1

"911 dispatcher to Pleasant Valley Police Department."
"Pleasant Valley PD. Go ahead 911."
"We have a report of a single gunshot from the Price cottage along Prince Gallitzin Lake. Do you need the address?"
"No thank you operator. I'm familiar with the residence."
"Good luck Pleasant Valley PD."

The lights on the top of the cruiser came to life and the siren wailed as the tires on the police cruiser fought a losing battle for traction. Eventually the twin black strips left on the asphalt came to a screeching halt and the cruiser rocketed away. Patrolman Shawn Boyer hustled the vehicle towards Prince Gallitzin Lake like a professional race car driver and he had good reason to be in a hurry. Dean "Cappie" Price was his friend. Dean actually lived next door to Shawn Boyer and "Cappie" had taught him the pleasures of canoeing. They spent most summer weekends paddling down a river somewhere in the tri-state area. Enjoying nature as they floated the flat water and getting exercise in the rapids. Most occasions they had other people with them. Dean may have been retired but as he was fond of saying, "Just because there is snow on the roof, that doesn't mean there's not a fire in the furnace." Cappie especially liked younger women and the feeling was mutual. The younger women liked him also. In fact most nights there was an extra car parked in front of Dean's house. Shawn spending plenty of weekends with Dean didn't hurt him any either as Dean always seemed to have an extra woman that needed an experienced canoeist to show her the ropes.

As the cruiser rounded the curve near the Price cottage, Shawn spotted a man with a golden retriever on a leash standing alongside the road. Seeing the flashing lights and hearing the siren the man began frantically waving his arms. Shawn stopped the car next to the man cutting off the lights and siren.

"Are you the gentleman that called 911?" Shawn asked.

"Yes. I was walking down by the lake in front of the Price cottage when I heard a gunshot."

"Are you sure it was a gunshot?"

"Yes, sir, I spend a lot of time at the range and I am very familiar with the sound of a gunshot."

"You say you heard one shot?"

"Yes, just one. Then I moved away from the property and called 911."

"Can I see some identification in case I need to get back to you?"

"Of course," the man said as he pulled out his wallet and handed Shawn his driver's license."

Shawn scribbled the information down then said, "Thank you. I'll be in touch if I have any questions."

The patrolman parked the cruiser where he was and walked the remaining distance to the cottage keeping his eyes peeled on the windows, his pistol out and pointing in the direction of

the cottage. Shawn went around the corner of the two story structure with the pealing white paint and quietly went up the steps to the deck and crossed over to the door. Shawn stood off to the side while he opened the rusted and broken screen door. He tried turning the handle on the main door. It turned so he shouted out, "Cappie, are you in there?"
No response.
He turned the door knob again and slowly opened the door. Scanning the dark interior and taking a fast peak around the corner of the door, Shawn crouched over and stealthily entered the house. He quickly checked the couple rooms on the first floor. No Cappie. He stopped at the bottom of the stairs and shouted, "Cappie, are you up there?"
No answer.
With his free hand he grabbed the banister and slowly started up the steps. Each step loudly protested his weight no matter how quiet he was trying to be. He stepped on the outside of each step and the creaking was a bit quieter. The staircase seemed unusually narrow to Shawn. Thoughts raced through his mind. *If someone came around the corner at the top of the staircase with a gun, he had nowhere to go. He was a sitting duck. A perfect target. The shooter wouldn't even have to be good to hit Shawn in the narrow staircase. Why didn't he call for back-up? Oh well, too late now.* Shawn had to press on to check on Dean. Each step was like an orchestra announcing his entrance. The armpits of his light blue uniform were soaked through as he reached the top step. Taking a breath he slowly peered around the corner. The words involuntarily left his mouth as he jerked back around the corner into the stairwell, "Oh shit."

Thank you Colleen for all your assistance.

Also by A. Wayne Ross:

QUARRY

OLD DOG, NEW TRICK

BLOOD ON THE RUNNING BOARDS

NO ONE NOTICED

WALK THE PLANK

THE GREATER GOOD

ANOTHER BLUE HOLE

BLUE HOLE

27027264R00052

Made in the USA
Columbia, SC
22 September 2018